THE
FIRE FIGHTERS'
COUNTING BOOK

By Polly Curren
Illustrated by Pat Stewart

A GOLDEN BOOK • NEW YORK
Western Publishing Company, Inc., Racine, Wisconsin 53404

This is the firehouse of Engine
Company Number 1.
All the fire fighters are busy.
In the kitchen, the Fire Chief
is mixing this and measuring that.
One Fire Chief, cooking.

Two fire fighters are whistling
while they work.
"Hey," says one, "I smell something good!"
"What's cooking, Chief?" asks the other one.
"It's a surprise," replies the Chief.
Two fire fighters, whistling and working.

Three fire engines are clean and shining.
There is one rescue truck...and one pumper...
and one hook-and-ladder.
Three fire engines, ready to go to work.
But first the fire fighters
must check their equipment.

3

There are four sharp axes.
Fire fighters need axes to get into
burning buildings.
Four axes, clean and polished.

There are five long hooks.
Fire fighters need hooks to pull down
ceilings in burning buildings.
Five hooks, ready for the hook-and-ladder.

6 Six round headlights sparkle on each engine.
Bright headlights light
the way for the fire engines at night.
Six headlights, round and sparkling.

ENGINE CO

7

There are seven strong, sturdy ladders.
Some are short. Some are long.
The very long one
on the top of the truck can reach up
seven floors to rescue people.
Seven ladders, strong and sturdy.

Eight hoses hang on the hose tower.
They are dry now, and
ready to go back on the pumper.
Eight hoses, all dry.

Nine fire dogs are romping in the firehouse.
The mother dog, the father dog,
and seven frisky puppies want to play with
the fire fighters.
"Woof! Woof!" they bark.
"We're too busy to play now," says one
fire fighter, laughing.
"Maybe after dinner, though."
Nine fire dogs, romping.

Ten happy fire fighters walk
into the kitchen. "We're ready
to eat," one says. "Woof! Woof!"
bark the excited puppies.
There on the table is a birthday
cake with a fat red candle
twinkling on it.

BIRTHDAY

"Surprise!" says the Chief.
"Engine Company Number 1
is one year old today.
Happy birthday, everyone!"
Ten fire fighters, celebrating.

10

Suddenly–*Clang! Clang! Clang!*
The fire alarm is ringing.
"That's us!" the Chief shouts. He blows
out the candle on the cake.
"Let's go," he says.
Up jump the fire fighters.
They race to their places.

On go their high boots.
The boots will keep the fire fighters' feet
dry when the hoses are used.
On go their rubber coats and hard helmets.
The coats and helmets will protect the
fire fighters from broken glass and other things
that might hurt them at the fire.

One fire fighter runs outside.
"Make way for the engines,"
he shouts to the people on the sidewalk.
The firehouse doors open wide.
The engines roar. The sirens screech.

Off goes Engine Company Number 1
to fight the fire.
"Woof," bark the dogs. They are left behind.
Down the street, a building is burning.
Flames are leaping out of the windows.

"Bring the hoses," one fire fighter shouts.
"Put up the ladders," another one yells.
"Get everyone out of the building,"
the Fire Chief orders.
The fire fighters work fast and
hard. Soon the fire is out.
All the people are safe.
"All clear," the Chief calls.
"Let's go back to the firehouse."

The tired, hungry fire fighters go back to the firehouse.
The puppies race to meet them, barking and jumping.
"Let's eat that birthday dinner," one fire fighter says.
"Let's play with the puppies," says another.
"Let's do both," the Fire Chief says. And they do.